The Girl Who Wore Snakes

story by Angela Johnson

paintings by
James E. Ransome

Orchard Books   New York

Orchard Books, 95 Madison Avenue,
New York, NY 10016

Manufactured in the
United States of America.
Printed by Barton Press, Inc.
Bound by Horowitz/Rae.
Book design by Mina Greenstein.
The text of this book is set in 18 point
Quorum Bold. The illustrations are oil on
paper reproduced in full color.

10 9 8 7 6 5 4 3 2 1

Library of Congress
Cataloging-in-Publication Data
Johnson, Angela. The girl who wore snakes /
by Angela Johnson ; paintings by
James E. Ransome.
p.   cm. "A Richard Jackson book"—Half-title.
Summary: Ali discovers that there is someone
else that thinks snakes are beautiful
and loves them as much as she does.
ISBN 0-531-05491-8
ISBN 0-531-08641-0 (lib. bdg.)
[1. Snakes—Fiction. 2. Pets—Fiction.
3. Aunts—Fiction. 4. Afro-Americans—
Fiction.]   I. Ransome, James, ill.
II. Title.   PZ7.J629Gi 1993 [E]—dc20
92-44521

To George Clinton and all
the members of Parliament / Funkadelic
for the music that inspires me
to reach inside and create

—J.E.R.

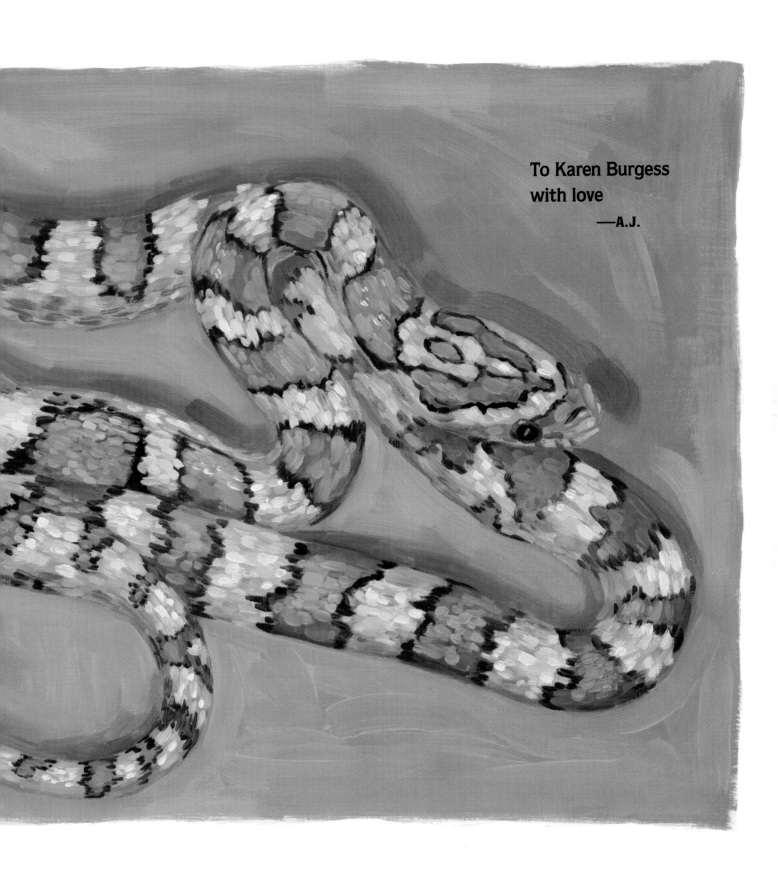

To Karen Burgess
with love

—A.J.

When the man from the zoo
came to Ali's school,
he brought Silvia, the snake.

She was brown, yellow, and orange,
and made Ali think of the sun
and the earth and everything
in between.

The zoo man said,
"Who wants to hold her?"

Ali said, "Me"—

and wore Silvia,
the brown, yellow, and orange snake,
all day long . . .

around her neck . . .
around her arms . . .
and around her ankles.

After Silvia went back to the zoo,
Ali became
the girl who wore the snake.

Then one day at the pet store
Ali became
the girl who bought all the snakes
and wore them home.

Her parents said,
"Why snakes? Why not dogs,
birds, cats, or fish?"
and they wondered
where she got her love of snakes.

Her friends said,
"Are you going
to wear those things
to the picnic?"

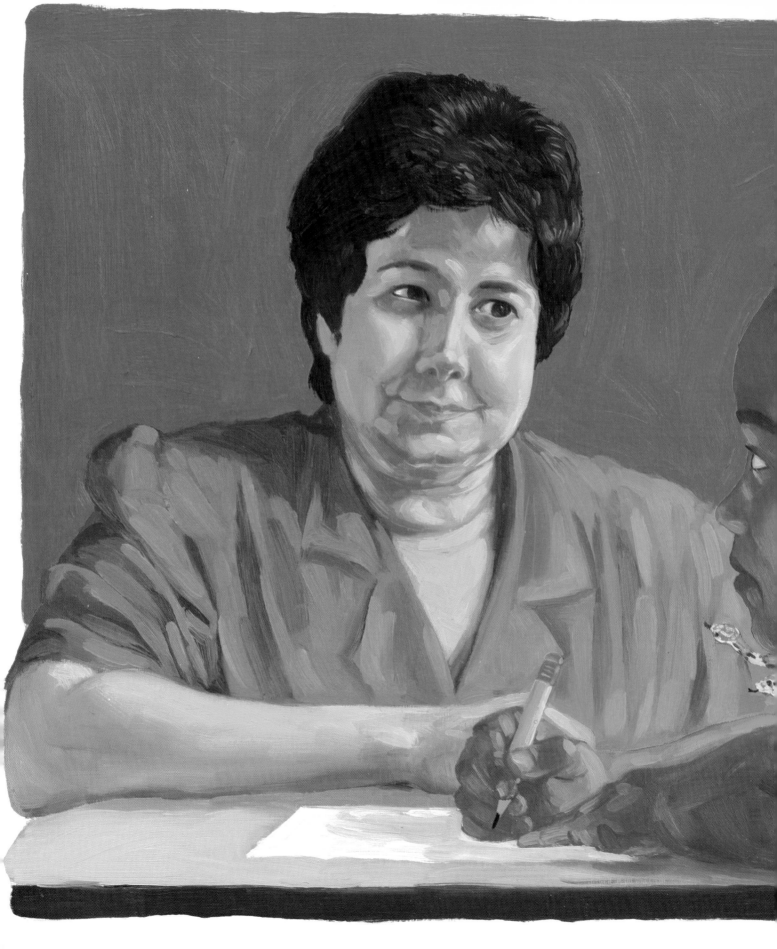

Her teacher said,
"Take the snakes off
during the test."

All of this was fine with Ali
because her snakes were
beautiful in the sun . . .
beautiful in the moon . . .
and even beautiful
in the windowsill of the kitchen.

But no one except Ali
could see
how beautiful they really were.

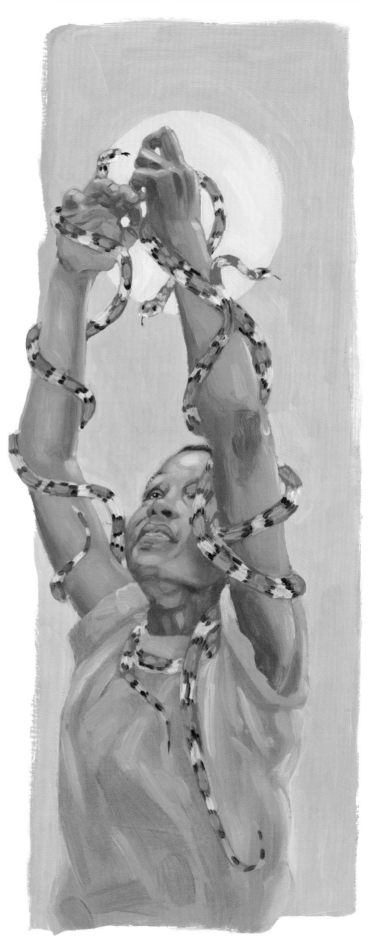

Until one day Ali went on vacation
to visit her old aunts.

The first one said,
"No snakes in the house."

The second one said,
"Don't they eat small animals?"

And the third one said,
"Nasty things."

But then the fourth aunt said,
"That one would look nice
around my arm, Ali.
It reminds me of the sun
and the earth and everything
in between. . . ."

Then Ali knew how she became
the girl who wore snakes . . .
around her neck . . .
around her arms . . .
around her ankles . . .

and thought again that they reminded her
of the sun and the earth
and everything in between.